FLaT
BroKe

ALSO BY GARY PAULSEN

GARY PAULSEN

FLaT BroKe

The Theory, Practice and Destructive Properties of Greed

WENDY
LAMB
BOOKS

Text copyright © 2011 by Gary Paulsen
Jacket art copyright © 2011 by James Bernardin

Visit us on the Web! www.randomhouse.com/kids
Educators and librarians, for a variety of teaching tools,
visit us at www.randomhouse.com/teachers

Library of Congress Cataloging-in-Publication Data
Paulsen, Gary.
  Flat broke / by Gary Paulsen.—1st ed.
     p.   cm.
  Summary: Fourteen-year-old Kevin is a hard worker, so when his income is cut off he begins a series of businesses, from poker games to selling snacks, earning money to take a girl to a dance, but his partners soon tire of his methods.
  ISBN 978-0-385-74002-9 (trade) — ISBN 978-0-385-90818-4 (lib. bdg.) — ISBN 978-0-375-89869-3 (ebook) — ISBN 978-0-375-86612-8 (pbk.)
  [1. Moneymaking projects—Fiction. 2. Business enterprises—Fiction. 3. Conduct of life—Fiction. 4. Friendship—Fiction. 5. Family life—Fiction. 6. Humorous stories.] I. Title.
PZ7.P2843F1 2011   [Fic]—dc22   2010049415

Printed in the United States of America
10 9 8 7 6 5 4 3 2 1
First Edition

*This book is dedicated
with appreciation and affection
to Sandy Weinberg,
my agent and good friend.*

Foreword

I'm the best worker you'll ever meet.

I should be good: I've had a lot of practice. I'm only fourteen, but I've known for as long as I can remember that you've got to do more than what's expected if you want to get ahead. It's a universal rule. A cosmic inevitability.

If you ask me, people who say you've got to work smart and not hard are just lazy.

I'm good because I give everything I do everything I've got.

See, people appreciate that kind of effort, and going the extra mile, I've found, always pays off.

"Kevin routinely applies himself, to the best of his abilities." That's what my teachers and counselors and coaches have always said. Whether it's scissor skills (I cut the straightest edges in the history of the Golden Valley Preschool) or tie-dying in summer camp (I raided my family's laundry basket and then twisted and rubber-banded and dyed everything white I could get my hands on— T-shirts, socks, shorts, my mother's bras, pillowcases, dish towels) or playing T-ball (where, although I lacked batting strength and only played an okay third base, I kept up the chatter and made the rest of the team sharp), I always do my best.

My grades aren't so amazing that people think I'm a prodigy or a cheat, but I'm in the top ten percent of my class and I always hand in a twelve-percent-higher page count than required for essay assignments. I'm the guy all my friends depend on to come up with a solid idea for what to do or crack a joke to lighten the mood. I'm the only person in my family who remembers to depoop our cat's litter box, which doesn't sound like a big deal, but it is to anyone who's ever smelled a ripe box.

Whatever I do, I do it well. Always have. It's just how I am.

I'm not bragging or conceited, I'm just telling it like it is.

I've usually gotten exactly what I wanted because I've always been willing to work hard.

I have a knack for knowing what needs to be said and done.

But it's easy to get into trouble with the details if you don't stay focused on the big picture.

Even though I know better, I forgot that bit for a while. Until my life turned into something like creamed chipped barf and peas on toast.

The Successful Person Can Make Something from Nothing

'd recently found myself in a world of trouble, because I used to lie. To everyone. About everything. All the time. But only because I was really good at it and lying made so much sense. Until my friends, family and teachers all got mad at me and I had to come up with about a hundred creative ways to apologize.

Things are better now. Except for the fact that I've got a serious cash problem. As in: I'm not making any.

My parents are teaching me a lesson: Since you lied, we're taking away your allowance for a month.

And even my weekend job working for my Auntie Buzz at her interior decorating business wasn't bringing in the money like it used to.

"Are you teaching me a lesson too? Because of the way I lied to you, um, to everyone?" I asked her after she told me I couldn't work for her for a month.

"No. I'm just mad at you."

I'm the kind of person who takes his punishment like a man, so I didn't even try to argue with her.

A guy's got to have some walking-around money, though, and I thought I could still count on babysitting money because I watch my four-year-old neighbor, Markie, once or twice a week. Markie was the only person I hadn't lied to, so I figured that income was safe.

"Hi, Dutchdeefuddy," Markie said, using his name for me. It means "best most favorite buddy in the world forever." As we waved goodbye to his mom on Sunday, he asked, "What does bankrupt mean?"

Last week I'd had to explain " 'vorces" to him because his parents were breaking up. And now, I guessed, going broke, too.

"What did you hear?" I asked. Markie might

have the attention span of a fruit fly, but he's got the hearing of a NASA deep-space probe.

"Mommy said they can't pay you or they'll go bankrupt."

Ah. Well. That figures.

Markie's folks were paying for the house and an apartment—Markie stayed put in the family home and his mom and dad moved in and out according to their custody schedule.

I hoped to keep my job. Markie needed me. Or I needed him. I hadn't figured that out yet. But there's something really nice about spending time with a little kid. You learn so much.

"Bankrupt means they don't have a lot of money right now," I said. "It's a grown-up thing, and you don't have to worry. I'm going to keep coming over like always, even if they can't pay."

"Cool."

Yeah, I thought, lack of money is the new in thing. "Hey, how about a banana dipped in melted chocolate chips?" He nodded and started peeling.

I am an excellent babysitter. Kids in my care get their three to five daily servings of fruit.

I shook some chocolate chips into a microwave-safe bowl and wondered: Why was the universe ganging up to make sure I didn't have any money?

Whoever says youth is the best time in your life has cash in hand and can't remember being poor.

My best friend, JonPaul, pounded on the door just as the microwave dinged. You know you've got a great friend when he doesn't mind hanging out with you when you're Markie-sitting.

"I'm starving." That's JonPaul's standard greeting. JonPaul is a jock, and it seems to me that he's on every team except girls' lacrosse, because he's always coming from practice or going to a game. I don't even know what season he's in; I can't keep track. "Let's order a pizza." He and Markie fist-bumped hello.

"Oh, uh . . . I'm a little short these days and . . ." I trailed off. JonPaul knew about my allowance penalty and how empty my pockets were.

"I got it," he said, and called the delivery place on his cell. I heard him order a vegetarian low-fat-cheese whole-wheat-crust pie and didn't feel so bad about not paying. JonPaul is a health nut and the food he eats is gross.

He'd been paying my way lately when we hung

out and he never said a word about me being a mooch, but still, it hurt my pride.

"Hey," JonPaul said after he and Markie had inhaled the pizza—I'd taken one look and made myself another banana with melted chocolate chips. "Did you hear that the new Death Rays of Mount Volupus IV game is coming out this week?"

I shrugged, trying to look like I didn't care, because I knew I wouldn't be able to afford it.

Markie and JonPaul started wrestling. Markie is small, even for a four-year-old, and JonPaul is ginormous because he's a gym rat and a jock and he works out all the time. But it wasn't even a close contest, because JonPaul is a little bit of a germaphobe. He pretended not to be bothered that Markie was all sticky and dirty with odds and ends of little-boy goo and snot, but he didn't put up much of a fight. Markie pinned him in seconds. As soon as Markie started parading around the living room with his arms in the air while I clapped for him, JonPaul rushed to the kitchen sink to disinfect. This made him forget all about the computer game and my money situation.

But *I* didn't forget. Every time I turned around,

it seemed, I was reminded how crummy life can be when you don't have spending money.

The final straw was the next day at school, when I saw a poster for a dance in a few weeks.

Not only did I want to go to that dance, I wanted to ask Tina Zabinski, the World's Most Beautiful Girl, to go with me. She was absolutely perfect. Well, except for a small freckle underneath her right eye that I'd noticed the other day when the light hit her face just right as she walked to the bus after school. It was the freckle that made me think I might stand a chance with her. Not quite perfect was more in my ballpark than totally flawless.

Ever since I'd suddenly noticed how gorgeous Tina was and realized how much I'd like to go out with her, I'd been striking out in terms of coming up with ways to impress her. But inviting her to the dance was a great idea. Girls like dances. I don't know why, I think they're horrible—my friends and I just hang around the refreshment table hoping we're not going to have to ask anyone to dance—but everything would be different if I walked in as Tina's date.

Just then, I saw a flash of blond hair outside the

cafeteria that could only belong to Tina. I decided to make my move.

I just hadn't expected that my move would be tripping over the janitor's bucket, spilling 700 gallons of filthy water on the floor. Which then cascaded down the southwest stairwell. The water picked up speed and, tsunami-like, wiped out a small group of sixth graders on the bottom step. I hung my head over the railing and watched them cartwheel off the step and land in a dingy puddle on the floor. I exhaled when one raised a hand to flash an "I'm-okay" thumbs-up.

As I slipped away from the gathering crowd and slunk down the hall to my next class, hoping no one would know I'd caused the flood and crash, I realized that it was just as well I hadn't been able to ask Tina to go to the dance with me—I couldn't afford the tickets yet.

Close call.

I had to find a way to make some money again. And pretty fast, too.

I'd read about a kid who started his own lawn-care service and became filthy, stinking rich. He made it look so easy.

Because my mother works in a bookstore, she brings home piles of books all the time. As soon as I got home from school, I dug through the shelves in the family room and pulled out all the business books. I've always liked reading about military history and have learned a lot about how to handle problems that way. The business books turned out to be kind of the same thing, except instead of generals, it's the chief operating officers who run the show. Same principle, though—divide, conquer, plunder, pillage, reap the spoils. Wash, rinse, repeat.

This was going to be great, I could just feel it. I wondered, though, why it had taken me until I was fourteen to think about getting rich. Better late than never, right? And after all, how many teenage gazillionaires are there? Getting rich would be helpful in making Tina realize how awesome her life would be once she became my girlfriend.

I was on track to win the girl of my dreams and get some money again.

I just had to figure out how.

The Successful Person Has Vision That Others Lack

I got my first idea when my buddies and I were playing poker during lunch the next day in a corner of the cafeteria. We didn't play for money, but for points.

"Points for what?" I finally asked JonPaul as we were leaving the cafeteria.

"We've been playing together since sixth grade and that's the way we've always done it," he answered. "We add up the points we've won and lost at the end of every hand, and I keep track of our overall winnings in my notebook." He held it up, like I'd never seen his ratty old notebook before.

"Yeah, I know, but don't you think we could make things more interesting if we played for money?"

"We can't bet money on school property."

"We'll play off school property, then."

"You don't have money," he reminded me.

"I could do something about that."

"Like what?"

"Start a poker game."

"We have a poker game."

JonPaul is a great friend, but he will never be business partner matcrial. The poor guy doesn't know how to think past the obvious to spot the potential the way I do. I'd thought it would be nice to be a team—me and JonPaul getting rich together. But I could already see that he'd be better off in a less ambitious position—more assistant than associate.

"Here's my plan: I organize a weekly poker game, for money, with the guys, away from school. I always win because they're terrible players, so that's a great way to turn a few dollars into more dollars. Then I figure out some other people who'd be interested in buying into other games. I'll set everything up—time and place—maybe give some pointers, and collect a buy-in fee from everyone, since it's my idea."

"How do you know about doing something like that?"

"I read a lot."

"You make it sound easy."

"What could be hard?"

Before he could answer, I peeled off and headed into class. I wasn't worried that JonPaul wasn't enthusiastic about my idea. He'd get on board eventually. That's the kind of friend he is.

During class, I thought about the guys I could hit up for my poker games and where I could hold them. My parents are pretty laid-back, but I figured even they might blow a gasket if I had people traipsing in and out of our basement on a regular basis.

One thing at a time. First the players, then the location.

Wheels. Dash. Jay M. They weren't very good, but I'd been playing with them since sixth grade and I knew they'd be glad to bet real chips, not those little paper flashcard things JonPaul came up with.

Wheels sat next to me in math, so I caught up with him as we were leaving class.

"Thinking about setting up a real poker game. For money. After school. You in?"

"Yup."

One of the great things about Wheels is that he never says more than necessary and he asks very few questions. Maybe that will get him in trouble someday, but it worked to my advantage right then.

I did my best Wheels impersonation and said, "Cool." Then I went to find Dash and Jay M. They were in and said they knew two guys from study hall who'd want to play too.

I approached my brother, Daniel, as soon as he got home from hockey practice that afternoon.

"You guys play any cards?" I asked before he even dropped his gear on the kitchen floor.

"No. Why?"

"Your team is together a lot. I just wondered how you passed the time."

He looked at me like I was half-witted and then gestured to his bag. "We play hockey."

"Well, yeah, sure. But a guy's got to have a hobby. Something fun to blow off steam. Your team takes hockey so seriously."

"Yeah, so?"

"I was thinking about setting up a poker game for you."

"Betting is a benchable offense."

"Oh. Well . . . Wait—Coach is probably referring to betting on the game."

"You think?" Daniel lives in fear that he'll tick off his coach and sit out a game. But he's a poker fiend. He's the one who taught me to play.

"Sure. Cards aren't the kind of betting he was talking about," I said.

"Maybe." Daniel sounded doubtful, but I could see that he was thinking about poker hands.

"Tell you what: I'll arrange everything. Gimme your schedule for the next couple of weeks and I'll tell everyone and get the cards and chips and set up a location. Coach'll never even know."

"I guess that sounds okay. Here." Daniel dug a crumpled wad of papers out of his duffel bag. "Team roster. And our schedule." He paused. "Why are you doing this? What's in it for you?"

"A small fee."

"Mom and Dad were serious about taking away

17

your allowance?" I nodded and he grinned. "Well, then, the poker game is a pretty good idea for everyone."

I'd traveled with the team before; Coach is always looking for volunteers to help carry bags and make coffee runs for him during away games, so I knew the guys. And I knew they'd be up for a game. They live to compete.

I sent out an email and before you know it, I had game number two set up.

I was a natural.

One of the books I'd read said that the savviest businesspeople always make plans in sets of three because that improves the odds of success.

So I called Goober, JonPaul's cousin, because he's in college and I figured he knew a bunch of guys who wouldn't mind spending some money on poker.

"Dude. You're smart for a little kid," he said. I let the little kid comment slide, but only because he'd started listing names. "There's Tommy and Pete and Ben and Chris and Jack. That's a start—four guys and me?"

"That's five guys plus you, Goob, but yeah, that'll work."

"Whatever. Counting's not my thing. Tomorrow would be great."

For a second I hoped his counting aversion didn't mean he couldn't identify numbers; I mean, there's only ten, nine if you count the ace as a face card and not as the one. Oh, what did I care? He wouldn't be playing with my money.

"Sure. Tomorrow. I'll get back to you later with the details."

Another book I'd read said you have to spend money to make money. Problem was: I didn't have any money. But I knew who did. And I could hear her car pulling into the driveway.

My sister, Sarah, makes me look like a petri dish full of pond sludge. I work hard, but she works all the time. She's sixteen, so she can drive, and as far as I can tell, all she does is drive to various part-time jobs and then to the mall to spend the money she's just earned. Except that I snuck a peek over her shoulder at her bank account summary on the family computer once and knew that she saved more than she spent.

"Hey, Kev, what's up?" she asked as she came into the kitchen. She must have been in a good mood, because she actually waited for my answer. Usually, when you talk to Sarah, you're speaking to the back of her head because she's always on the move.

"Not much."

"Why are you just sitting there?" She dumped her backpack on the table to start her homework.

"Waiting for you."

"I can't drive you anywhere until after I've finished my reading assignment and an essay and this page of math problems."

"I don't want a ride."

"What do you want?"

"Money."

"How much? And why? And you know I don't just give money away for nothing. There's a vig."

I raised my eyebrows, glad that one of the books I'd read had been written by a guy in the witness protection program, explaining his former career as a loan shark. I knew that a vig was the interest due on money borrowed. My sister is a dark and mysterious person. More likely, she read the same book in our basement. I was starting to like her more and more.

"I need fifty dollars, and I'll pay you back tomorrow."

"I'll still have to charge you five bucks, though."

"Deal."

She gave me the money and I biked to the If We Don't Have It, You Don't Need It store to get cards and chips. I'm a class act—none of those sticky cards from the family room.

I also filled a cart with huge bags of pretzels and bottles of soda. Everything runs smoother with a snack. I know that from babysitting Markie. I was willing to bet there wasn't a whole lot of difference between a four-year-old, some eighth graders, a high school hockey team and undergrads. Guys like munchies.

As I biked home from the store with a backpack full of pretzels hanging from my shoulders, and another backpack, baby carrier–style on my chest, full of soda, and two plastic bags of cards and chips hanging from the handlebars, I thought about my next step.

I had the players. I had the supplies. Now I had to find a place to hold the games.

Examine the facts. That's what smart business-people do.

Fact #1: Auntie Buzz owns a small building downtown that houses her decorating business. Fact #2: It sits empty a lot of the time because she's either at a job site or at some store buying pillows and crown molding. Fact #3: She's got a conference table with lots of chairs. Fact #4: Kevin needs convenient space with a table.

I dumped the poker supplies in my room and turned my bike in the direction of Auntie Buzz's office. I rode a lot faster than when I'd been carrying all the supplies.

"Auntie Buzz."

She looked up from her desk, started to smile, remembered she was still mad about the way I'd lied to her, and scowled.

"I'm here to make you an offer," I said.

"I have an MBA, I'm wired on too much caffeine and I have a grudge against you. You think you have what it takes to do business with me?"

"Yup."

"I'm a sucker for self-confidence. State your case."

"I need to sublet space from you because I'm starting a business."

"What kind?"

"Um, it's, well, still in the early stages. I don't want to say too much too soon and jinx it, but I need room to, uh, for, like, meetings. And stuff."

"It's the 'stuff' that worries me."

"I'll pay you rent."

Auntie Buzz just studied me. Finally, she spoke.

"I'm not so sure I believe you're about to launch a worldwide conglomerate, but your presence will deter rodents. I've noticed mouse droppings lately. Fine. You can borrow my conference room when I don't have client meetings."

"Great."

"We'll talk money after a brief probationary period to see if this works."

"Thanks."

"Break anything, get anything dirty, leave food around, touch anything in this office except for the doors, the floor and the table, and I will rain misery on you."

"You won't even know we were here."

"I doubt that very much. But I'm curious to see what kind of business you come up with."

I ignored her skeptical tone. I'd read that every great businessperson has had to overcome doubters. It's practically a law. So Auntie Buzz was already validating my future success.

The first game was right after school the next day, with Wheels and the guys. I dealt and then watched them mess up a few hands. Finally, I couldn't keep my mouth shut any longer. I put down my hand.

"Wheels, you bet high when you should fold."

He looked furious. "It's called bluffing."

"You're terrible at it. Stop."

For a second he looked like he was going to punch me, but then he glanced at his meager pile of chips and held still.

"Jay," I went on, "you get scared when the pot gets above five dollars."

"Do not."

"Do too. Man up or leave the game. You can't think about the money. That's the secret."

"I liked it better when we played for points. Money makes me nervous."

"Once you win, you'll like playing for money way better than playing for points."

Jay M. fiddled with his chips and looked unconvinced. I turned to Dash, who had been studying the other players' faces rather than his hand.

"Dash, you're too sure you can read everyone's tells. But that just makes you forget your own cards."

"I'm good at reading people."

"That doesn't help if you've got a crappy hand."

I didn't know the other two guys, Nolan and Collin, very well. But they were careful players, and they didn't make mistakes. JonPaul had a meet. Or a match. Or practice. Whatever. He'd said he couldn't make the poker game. I think the real reason was that he didn't want to touch the germy cards.

I watched them play another five or six hands, s-l-o-w-l-y because they were all thinking so hard. But they were getting better, not to mention more comfortable betting—and winning—money. I circled the table, giving advice and making sure everyone won a hand or two so that they got the taste of a win. That would keep them coming back for more.

Finally, I had to kick them out because my second game was going to start in fifteen minutes. Since I'd dropped out of the game and had started offering advice, not to mention that I'd found the location and supplied the snacks, I explained that it was only fair that I take a cut of their winnings. They were surprisingly okay with that idea. If you say things the right way, people are almost happy about giving you their money.

As soon as they left, I hustled around Auntie Buzz's conference room. I set out a new deck of cards, restacked the chips, organized a new batch of refreshments and straightened the chairs. I even ran the vacuum cleaner around the room to suck up the pretzel crumbs. It's the little things that make the big difference.

Daniel's teammates may be scary on the ice, but they're mellow when they take their skates off. Everyone bought in and settled down to the hand quickly. There must be something to Coach's discipline, because they were all strong players. They didn't need my help.

So I poured soda, handed around snacks, explained how to set aside the house's earnings at the end of the game (the house—that's me; cool) and left for Goober's dorm room.

For college guys, they were as dumb as mold.

They were all really jazzed to play, but they didn't know spit about the game. I had to explain the basics. Several times.

"A straight beats a pair or three of a kind," I said.

"Wait! I know that one!" Chris said. "A straight is when the cards are in order."

I nodded. "And a flush, a hand that's all one suit, beats a straight." Confused looks. "A suit is diamonds or hearts, which are red, or clubs, which look like black clovers, or spades, which look like . . . well, they're the other black suit."

Nods.

"A full house, which is three of a kind and a pair, beats a flush." They'd started taking notes.

"Four of a kind beats a full house," I continued.

"And five of a kind beats that!" Tommy beamed.

"You can't have five of a kind; four is the max. But I like the way you're thinking, Tom. A straight flush, which is cards in numerical order in the same suit, beats four of a kind. And a royal flush, which is the five highest cards in a suit—the ace, king, queen, jack, and ten—beats everything."

The good thing was that they weren't embarrassed that they didn't know anything about playing cards.

I helped them play for a few hands ("Stop dealing after everyone has five cards, Goob") and then walked out to the front steps of the dorm to reflect on my first day as a genuine, moneymaking businessman.

The first three games had trucked along, and I already had a pretty good wad of cash in my pocket. The next step was going to be figuring out a discreet way to let Tina know I was fast on my way to becoming a mogul. She didn't seem like the kind of girl who'd be impressed by money, but I thought she'd be interested in any guy who worked as hard as I did.

I had told my mom I was working—vague, but no lie—so I'd missed dinner while I was getting the first three games off the ground. But sacrifice, I had read, is part of any success. I headed home to see if there were any bananas and chocolate chips left. A celebration dinner.

The Successful Person is a Creative Thinker

I knew the poker games would be good for some steady cash. And I thought: If the poker games were that easy to set up, I should come up with other ideas. Because now that I had a taste for making money, I—well, I had a taste for making money.

I'm not a jock like JonPaul and Daniel the hockey prodigy, I don't fart rainbows like my parents seem to think Sarah does, and other than the lying thing, I'm pretty low-maintenance. I think it's easy to overlook a guy like me; I could be taken for granted. Being self-sufficient doesn't really call attention to itself.

I get along with my dad, but we don't have a lot in common. And actually, I have never truly figured out what my dad does for a living. I know he's the vice president of long-range strategic planning for an investment firm, but I don't really know what that means. He tried to explain once, but when he threw out the term *theoretical precepts*, he lost me.

But maybe we did have something in common: we were both businessmen.

It was starting to look like this moneymaking talent was my special skill. Something that would make everyone, especially Tina, realize how unique I really am. And it would give me a lot of interesting things to say to people, like Dad. Let's face it, summarizing your day in the eighth grade doesn't make for the best conversation ("I stared at Tina. All day. It made me sweat in funny places"). But talking about my business strategy—well, who wouldn't want to hear about that?

The more I thought about it, the more sense it made to throw everything I had into making as much money as I could while I was still in middle school.

I wasn't a dopey kid anymore; it was time to get

serious about my future. A whatchamacallit, a financial empire, was not out of the question if I worked hard enough.

I looked up from the notes I was jotting at my desk at corporate HQ.

Technically, HQ was an unused storage closet at the back of Auntie Buzz's office. I needed a real office if I was truly going to be someone important. I sat a little taller in the chair behind the three-legged desk I'd rescued from the Dumpster in the alley and propped up with sample books of curtain fabric. The file folders in front of me were empty, but I labeled them anyway—ACCOUNTS RECEIVABLE, CLIENT DATABASE, PENDING TRANSACTIONS.

I straightened a photo of my house that I'd put in a frame and set on my desk. I'd read that the best leaders never forget where they came from. My modest beginnings. That was how I'd refer to my childhood home during interviews someday.

Okay.

Brainstorming. How a fourteen-year-old guy like myself could make more money.

Quick money.

Big money.

Constant money.

I started by listing all the usual ways: baby-sitting, yard work, a lemonade stand, car washes.

I used to do okay Markie-sitting, but other than him, I don't really know many little kids. He's my next-door neighbor, so I started babysitting him, but in general I'm not that interested in little kids. Markie's more like a little brother or a little me than a kid, anyhow.

The book about the guy with the lawn service was a downer, because I was already doing yard work for my parents. For free. Part of the If You Lie, Bad Things Will Happen program at the Spencer homestead.

The lemonade stand had potential, but only if I did something to make the idea more special, more me-like. I put an asterisk next to that one for further study.

Car wash? Nope. The high school cheerleading squads had the corner on that market. There was no way I could compete with teenage girls in shorts and swinging ponytails.

Ponder, ponder, ponder.

I'd always thought I'd be good at creating television shows. I had dozens of ideas for game shows, reality programming, sitcoms, hourlong dramas, documentaries, talk shows. I could fill a week's worth of airtime with all my great ideas.

But my parents are always going on about TV sucking the life out of a person's mind and depriving that person of IQ points, and I didn't want to start out my career disappointing my folks. Plenty of time for that later. When they can no longer ground me or take away my allowance.

Think: What does a fourteen-year-old want?

Pictures of girls in bikinis. Mini-bikinis. Skin.

If the fourteen-year-old is a male.

I wondered how hard it would be to produce a calendar. And then I imagined how much fun it would be to hold a casting call for models in swimsuits showing lots of skin.

I put that idea in a FUTURE PLANS folder, along with the TV mogul idea. For when I could, you know, talk to girls without falling over my own feet every time I tried to open my mouth.

Like with the Three Bears, I knew there had to

be something that was Just Right for Kevin. But the brilliant plans weren't coming as easily as I'd expected.

Take a break. Let the ideas find me.

I took a deep cleansing breath, like my mom taught me during her yoga phase. She spent a lot of time standing with one foot on the other thigh and her hands in prayer position at her heart. Then I wrote BUSINESS PLAN on the top of the list and signed my name on the bottom: *Kevin L. Spencer.*

Middle initials are cool. I wished I was a Jr. or, better yet, a III or even a IV. Or was K. Lucas Spencer cooler?

I straightened my file folders, proud of my efforts on the crucially important first day of the rest of my life. Good work, Kev! I didn't mind complimenting myself, since there was no one else around to do it, and praise, I'd read, keeps people motivated.

I wasn't even too bummed that I still hadn't figured out a way to bring up the subject of my soon-to-be-wealthdom with Tina.

The Successful Person Knows That Hard Work, Although Not Necessarily His Own, Is the Cornerstone of His Achievements

The following morning I went to school without a plan for getting rich, but with a better idea about how to build my business. It had come to me while I was sleeping. I'd dreamed that I had a butler and a chauffeur and a cook and a personal trainer. And I woke up knowing that what was missing was a staff.

Sometimes you have to work backwards. So I'd focus on hiring people to work for me, and eventually, the idea of what we could actually all be doing would make itself known. Momentum was probably more important than specifics—right?—in starting up.

JonPaul was waiting for me by the front door of school.

"I want to get rich," I said right away. One of the books said repeating your objective helps you achieve it.

JonPaul hadn't read that book. "You already told me that."

"The poker games are just the first step."

"In what?"

"My business plan."

"Oh . . . sure. How's that coming along?"

"Great. I know just what I need."

"What's that?"

"People."

"Excuse me?"

"I should have people."

"But you don't."

"But I should. Get me some."

"Okay."

"That can be your first job: hiring employees."

"For what?"

"My business."

"What business? Did you figure that out?"

"Not all the way. But I will. Don't worry. I have a plan."

He started laughing. "You're the only fourteen-year-old guy I know who plans to rule the world."

"*Run* the world, JonPaul, *run*, not rule. And I do not. I just want to get filthy, stinking rich. The sooner the better. Because that's the American Dream. Or the Puritan work ethic. It's . . . something patriotic and ambitious."

I could tell he didn't really understand what I was talking about. Few do. But JonPaul is the kind of friend who will help.

He knows more people than anyone I'd ever met. He's on good terms with everyone at our school and has friends at Sandberg, our rival school, as well as the Catholic middle school.

I'd been at HQ for an hour or so after school that day when he poked his head through the door.

"I found you people!"

I tried to look as if I had expected him to be this successful this fast.

"Great! Way to go! Let's meet them."

"It's not a *them*, it's a *she*."

Oh.

I rallied. "Good. That was smart, JonPaul; we don't want to bring too many people on board all at once."

"Right! That's what I thought. Sam!" he called.

Sam was a tiny girl with curly red hair and enormous green eyes and she couldn't have weighed eighty pounds if she'd been soaking wet and holding a large houseplant. She looked thrilled and hopeful, like she was about to do something amazing, instead of hooking up a part-time job working for an eighth grader.

"HiI'mSamit'sSamanthareallybuteveryonehas alwayscalledmeSamwhichisaboy'snameeventhough I'magirl."

Whoa. I think and talk fast, but this girl was in hyperdrive, the kind that made the speed of light seem sluggish by comparison.

"Hi, Sam; I'm Kevin. Why don't you tell me a little bit about yourself and why you think you're right for this position?" She opened her mouth, but I cut her off. "Slowly. We don't pay by the word."

38

She nodded eagerly. "Right. I talk fast when I get nervous and this is my first job interview, so I'mreallyanxious."

I smiled sympathetically. I wasn't about to tell her it was my first job interview too.

"I'm thirteen, I go to the Aubrey Conley Day School, I'm an only child, I like sushi, I hate olives, and math is my best subject. I volunteer at the hospital and I babysit for the neighbors, but Idon'thavearealjob.Notajoblikewhatyou're offering."

She had promise, this wee lass. Even if she did talk reallysuperfast.

I saw her study the workstations—my desk, a cracked coffee table and a bedside stand with a huge scratch. Seating consisted of a dining room chair with a stain, and a wooden crate. Nothing matched, but I liked how the furniture filled up the storage closet, even though you had to climb over my desk to enter or leave the office.

"I like what you've done with your place," she said. "It's the sign of a guy who's not afraid to take risks and doesn't play by the rules."

This girl had a good head on her shoulders. And

if the longest journey begins with one small step, then my future empire would begin with one tiny worker.

"You're hired. Any curfew restrictions we need to worry about with your folks?"

"No, as long as I'm with you and JonPaul and I'm home by nine, they're okay."

"How do you two know each other, anyway?"

Sam ducked her head, and JonPaul, I swear, blushed.

Oh.

"Wemetattheallergist'soffice."

"How long ago was that?"

"We'vebeengoingtogetherforafewweeks."

Uh-huh.

"Where's the john?" JonPaul asked. Probably nervous because I'd just met his girlfriend. The girlfriend he hadn't told me about.

"Do that on your own time, okay? Captains of industry don't pee."

"How do you know these things, Kev?"

"I do my research."

"Do advisors pee?"

"Yes, but only after meetings. And you're not an advisor. You and Sam are staff."

"Oh," Sam said sadly. "Just staff."

JonPaul looked at her like she was the greatest idea since melted chocolate chips and bananas.

JonPaul. In love. With a chatty, smart munchkin. Color me surprised.

I hoped I wouldn't have to draft a policy about employees not dating. Nah. Until it became an issue that affected productivity or got really uncomfortable, I'd turn a blind eye to the, uh, interoffice, um, romance.

Speaking of romance, if JonPaul could get a girlfriend before he even had this nifty job working for me, surely I could get Tina to be my girlfriend once I told her about the business and the employees and all the ideas I had for getting rich. I just had to figure out how to bring all this to her attention without looking like I was bragging—or boring. Some people, after all, aren't business-minded. I didn't think Tina was like that, though; she always seemed really smart to me.

I left JonPaul and Sam sitting together on the

crate talking about allergy shots and organic fruit juices. Time to find Tina. The clock was ticking toward the dance. Get her to say yes before someone else asks her!

I knew that Tina took Irish dance lessons three doors over from Auntie Buzz's office and that if I timed it right, I could "accidentally" run into her while she waited for her mom to pick her up in the parking lot.

I walked down the street toward the dance studio. A bunch of girls came out and started heading toward me. Before I could even tell if Tina was with them, I panicked and jumped into the alley to hide. I needed a minute to compose myself, find the right words for Tina. I was crouched by the Dumpster, thinking, when a pair of sparkly pink gym shoes appeared in my line of vision.

"Hi, Kev. What're you doing?" Tina asked. She didn't look like she thought it was weird that I was lurking in a grungy alley by the garbage. No, she was smiling. Even as I wanted to die of embarrassment, the thought flashed through my head that she was a one-in-a-million kind of girl to be so cool about talking to a guy sitting next to a smelly garbage bin.

I stood up. I *tried* to stand up. I *meant* to stand up, but my legs must have fallen asleep while I was hunched down. I lost my balance on my numb legs and I . . . teetered. And tipped right over onto Tina. I'm not a big guy, but I fell hard and she wasn't expecting it and I knocked her right over. Flat on her back on a pile of crumpled cardboard boxes to be recycled, with me right next to her.

She wasn't mad or upset at all—even though I'd Flat Stanleyed her in a grimy alley and was now kind of frozen and couldn't seem to make myself move away from her. She laughed and said, "Are you okay? I didn't mean to surprise you like that."

How . . . soft she was and how nice it would be to stay here in the alley until I came up with all the right and perfect words to tell her how incredible I thought she was and how badly I wanted her to feel the same way about me. And I was thinking maybe that should be my new plan, staying here with Tina forever, when I was yanked to my feet by a hand on the back of my belt. JonPaul hauled me up and away from Tina like he was picking up a rag doll.

"Ohmygoshareyouokay?" Sam extended a hand to Tina and helped her up too. "Wasitarobbery attemptinbroaddaylight?"

"I'm okay, and we weren't being mugged. I . . . I tripped, and Kev tried to catch me, but I knocked him down too." Tina laughed again and brushed herself off while I thought: I could go right ahead and die here and now. Life couldn't possibly get any better than having Tina cover for me.

"*You* fell?" JonPaul didn't try to hide his skeptical tone.

"Yes, I was running out of dance class and wasn't paying attention and I ran right into Kev."

She gave me a look. One of those looks that make you turn hot and cold and sweaty and cotton-mouthed all at the same time. "I'm having a bad week," she continued. "The other day I dumped over the janitor's bucket and nearly drowned some sixth graders on the southwest stairs."

I opened my mouth to thank her for not making me look like an idiot in front of JonPaul and Sam and to apologize for the waterfall I'd been responsible for and to tell her how awesome she was to be taking the heat for me and that I wanted to send her flowers and open doors and throw my jacket on top of mud puddles for her to walk over and a million and one other great and romantic things that were roaring through my head. It came out, "Puddles."

She didn't even look surprised. And she must speak blithering idiot, too, because she said, so only I could hear, "Our secret," and then, more loudly for Sam and JonPaul, "Oh, there's my mom. Anyone need a ride?"

"Yesthanksifit'snotoutofyourway," Sam said, and dragged JonPaul after her to climb into the car that had just pulled up to the curb.

I tried to nod, I meant to nod, I wanted to nod, but some wires in my brain must have gotten crossed when I fell, because I felt myself shaking my head.

Tina waved as she got into the front seat, and then her mother pulled away, leaving me standing in the middle of the sidewalk. Where the wires got uncrossed and I blurted a perfectly good speech to no one but a golden retriever that'd been sitting by a parking meter.

"I think you're the most beautiful girl I've ever met, I'm starting a business to try to impress you and I'd like to ask you to go with me to the dance that's coming up soon," I said in a perfectly normal voice.

"Woof." The golden retriever wagged her tail.

Well, it was a start. My line worked on the dog, and Tina and I had shared A Moment, A Look and Two Helpful Lies. What a girl! Next time: no falling and no gurgling.

The next time I talked to Tina, everything was going to click into place.

5

The Successful Person Is
a Carpe Diem Kind of Guy

Hiring Sam earlier that afternoon had given me food for thought. If I could make good use of employees, maybe I could partner up with other successful people.

I walked home from The Moment with Tina and studied my family over the dinner table. I'd already decided my parents were nonstarters in terms of ideas to exploit—my mother manages a bookstore and is always saying there's no money in what she does, that working on behalf of literacy is a labor of love. And I wanted to impress my dad, not ask him for help being impressive.

I studied Daniel and Sarah over my mac-and-cheese casserole and green beans. Nothing came to me as I watched them chew.

As soon as dinner was over, Sarah headed to her place of worship. Our/her bathroom.

As I've mentioned, my sister, Sarah, is sixteen. And vain. My mother says that's typical of a girl her age. Daniel and I think it's typical of a pain in the butt, because we share a bathroom with her.

Our/her bathroom is more or less equidistant from all three bedrooms. I measured; I'm three-sixteenths of an inch closer than Daniel, but Sarah is directly across the hall from the bathroom, which we are *supposed* to share with each other.

There are three sets of hooks for towels and three separate plastic bins under the sink for each of us to keep our stuff in. But Sarah has taken over all the drawers and the counter space around the sink. Which is where she keeps hot, spiky hair-fixing things that hurt.

Her showers take forever, and I think she sleeps in the bathroom too. Probably hanging upside down by her heels from the shower rod because it's some beauty secret she read about.

And she's always having her coven over before parties and dates and sporting events to do their makeup and fix their hair.

Daniel finally gave up on trying to use our/her bathroom and troops down to the basement to use the funky, leaky shower that Dad installed in the laundry room, which smells like monkey butt.

I resort to drastic measures like licking Sarah's makeup, powdering my unmentionables with her makeup brushes and flushing the downstairs toilet while she's in the shower.

But that night, watching Sarah head into the bathroom to plug in a flatiron when I knew she wasn't going out, I got curious about girls and their addiction to beauty routines. The next day after school, I trotted down to the closest beauty salon and sat in the front, pretending to be waiting for someone. I studied what went on and I listened to the rip of the credit card scanner as everyone paid.

On the way home, I stopped by a beauty supply store and used some of my poker money to buy Sarah a tall director's chair, a three-sided, lighted countertop mirror and an electric hot wax pot. I lugged everything home. Did Bill Gates or Donald

Trump or Sam Walton or any of those other hugely successful business guys ever go to this much trouble for supplies?

As soon as I got home, I set everything up in our/her bathroom and sat working at my computer and waiting for Sarah to appear.

"What's with the stuff in her bathroom, Kev?" Daniel asked after hockey practice.

"Part of my Master Plan," I said mysteriously.

Daniel shrugged. "Hey, I'm supposed to tell you: the guys like grape soda and we want tortilla chips, not pretzels, next time."

I nodded and made a note. I'd started carrying a notebook around with me so that I could jot down great ideas. Or shopping lists.

"What's with the stuff in my—I mean, *our* bathroom?" Sarah asked when she got home.

"I'm helping."

"Helping what?"

"You. You already have what amounts to a beauty parlor in our bathroom."

She stared at me with slitted eyes.

"When your friends come over, they have to sit on the countertop, the mirror over the sink doesn't have magnification, and you've been buying little jars of wax to melt in the microwave in the kitchen. I bought you a client chair, a lighted mirror and a salon-grade wax pot that plugs in. More volume."

"Why?"

"I upgraded your skinny butt and—"

"You think my butt's skinny?" She twisted around to try to see her rear end.

"—and so it's only fair that I, um, reap part of the profits."

"What profits?"

"What are you talking about?" Even Daniel had started paying attention.

"Your friends need to start paying you. You've been doing their hair and makeup for free. Charge them."

"But, Kevin, they're my *friends*. I can't ask them for money. That'd be gross."

"What's gross is the way you run your business."

"My . . . I'm doing makeup for my girlfriends. That's not a business."

"Everything's a business."

"You're repellent."

"Whatever. I've, um, enhanced your resources. I

51

should, uh, see some, whattayoucallit, benefits from my . . . investment."

"What?"

"I want a cut."

"You're a greasy little bully, you know that?"

"You've been a bathroom hog for years, and now I've figured out how to make some money from it."

"But—"

"Look, Sarah, are you a charity or are you a, a, an enterprise in the making?"

"What are you talking about!"

"Making money."

She opened her mouth to answer and was cut off by the doorbell. Mom answered the door. It was Connie Shaw, my debate buddy. She of the Scary Monobrow.

"Sarah. Have you met Connie?" Sarah's face lit up when she caught sight of Connie's eyebrow. And the twenty Connie had clutched in her hand. "I told her you were a beauty whiz."

"There's more where that came from," I whispered to Sarah after she got Connie settled in her director's chair in front of the mirror and plugged in the wax pot.

She looked sympathetic. "Yeah, eighth grade is a tough time in a girl's life. But zipzip that brow and she's gorgeous." Sarah patted my arm. "Leave it to me, Kev, I've got this covered."

"Give me your client list."

"My what?"

"Your address book."

"Why?"

"I took a good look at the computer at the beauty salon and was able to replicate the calendar system they use for making appointments. I'll start calling your clients and getting them on a routine."

She shook her head and started to speak, but I cut her off. "I also set up an email address where everyone can ask for time slots. You won't have to do a thing but makeup and hair. Which you're doing anyway. And collect the money."

Sarah looked at me the way I've seen her study the gobs of gunk my father pulls from the shower drain. "You are a piece of work, you know that?"

"I'm your agent. And don't forget that you've got a client sitting in your chair. Remember the upsell—ask if she wants to try out other services you provide. We'll talk about my commission later. Don't worry, it's reasonable."

I walked back to my room, thinking it was kind of too bad that Tina's already perfect. Everything about her is just right—I don't know how tall she is, but it seems like she's not too tall and not too short. Blond hair with about a hundred different shades of gold, eyes that are this blue-green or green-blue, I can't tell, but I'm sure there's not even a name for it. Someday I'll have to invent the names to describe her hair and her eyes.

There's not a single thing on her that needs fixing except maybe the freckle, or Sarah's new salon would be a great way to get her into my house. But Connie's one of her best friends, and I'm sure Tina will be pleased Connie's not rocking the monobrow any longer and then she'll ask Connie what happened and Connie will tell her that I saved her from ugliness and Tina will realize that I'm not just clumsy and tongue-tied, but very thoughtful, too.

So, yeah, Tina will start to think good things about me and that's when I'll swoop in and tell her what I told the golden retriever.

I love it when my plans start to come together.

The Successful Person Finds Gold in What Others Consider Dross

JonPaul and I rode our bikes to the hot dog stand for a bite on Saturday. It's the only time of the week when JonPaul's not counting carbs and calories and sugar grams; usually he eats organic, free-range, preservative-free food. But Saturdays he pigs out with me. It's great. A real bonding experience.

We weren't really hungry, so we just had a light snack. Jumbo dogs, fully loaded—mustard, relish, sport peppers, extra onions, tomatoes, celery salt—with a couple of sides of extra-large chili-cheese fries and handcut onion rings. Amazing belches. Ah-may-zing.

"I think we overdid the onions today, JonPaul. Because I can't smell anything anymore."

He shrugged, sniffed and said, "Weird, huh?"

We were sitting on the curb, licking the last of the hot-dog ooze off our fingers, when shouts came from the storage facility across the parking lot.

JonPaul, although wussy about his health, is really brave. He jumped up and hustled over. I sighed and followed. Slowly. Hoping that everything would be resolved by the time I got there.

Turns out some guy hadn't paid his rent because management hadn't prevented some mama raccoon from having her babies—her un-potty-trained babies—in his storage locker, ruining his tent and hiking boots and anorak.

"Look, pal, you gotta clean out your own locker," the manager bellowed.

"I'm not touching that stuff—this is your responsibility," the renter hollered back.

"I'll touch it," I said.

"You'll what?" They turned to me.

"Yeah, sure, I'll clean it out for you; how bad can it be?"

"You've never smelled raccoon urine."

"I can't smell anything; I think the onions on the hot dog I just ate burned out my smell sensors or something."

JonPaul peered into the space. "Looks like a one-man job, Kevin. I'm gonna head off now and catch you later." He jogged away.

He'd probably read about germs and wild animals. Now he'd gone home to plunge his entire body into a large vat of disinfectant. I shrugged and turned back to my new job.

I have never seen two happier faces than on those guys. They offered me a hundred bucks to empty the locker and drag the contents to the Dumpster. The manager loaned me some work gloves, and they went to the office to sign papers.

It only took me twenty-five minutes to throw everything away. I couldn't smell a thing, but my eyes were watering and I itched where the wild-animal pee had come into contact with my skin.

I collected my cleaning fee and headed home to disinfect. A hundred dollars, and it was still early afternoon on a Saturday.

On my way, I walked past Mrs. Middlebrook, out in front of her house. She waved me over.

"Kevin, I'll give you fifty dollars to do to my garage what you did to that storage locker. I saw you cleaning it out as I drove by."

"I just threw everything away."

"You drive a hard bargain, my young friend, but okay, seventy-five dollars, and that's my final offer."

I peeked inside her garage. Unlike in the storage space, I didn't see any barfed raccoon goo or other clumps of crud that would have meant animals had nested there.

"Mrs. Middlebrook, you've got yourself a deal. I'm going to need some large plastic trash bags, work gloves and a bunch of cardboard boxes."

She nodded in the direction of a pile of supplies in the corner, jumped into her car, which was standing in the driveway (it didn't fit in the garage because of all the clutter) and drove off.

Turns out I like getting rid of junk. I found an old radio in the first layer and turned it on. The music was blaring, the sun was shining, and I was finding floor and wall surface that hadn't been exposed to fresh air in decades. I just dragged everything to the end of the driveway and made neat piles for the garbage truck to pick up.

When I was done, Mrs. Hedrick from across the street asked what my price was to clean her garage. I screwed up my face and scrunched my eyes in what I hoped looked like the intense concentration of an experienced professional.

"Let's see," I muttered, just loudly enough for her to hear, "the structure is, say, twenty by twenty, and . . ."

We haggled for a few minutes and I headed into her garage. I took Mrs. Middlebrook's former radio with me.

An hour later I was squaring up the last of the piles at the end of Mrs. Hedrick's driveway when her husband drove up. Mr. Hedrick looked perplexed when he saw me. He looked worried as he studied the piles. When he saw his beautiful, cavernous, spotless garage, his face turned bright red.

"You threw everything away."

"Not everything; I hung the tools back up on the pegs on the pegboard and I left the lawn mower and the trash cans against the far wall."

"But the boxes . . ."

"How important could that stuff have been, anyway?"

"There were items of great sentimental value."

"They're still sitting on the driveway wrapped in papers that predated the moon shot."

"Young man, I don't think you appreciate the seriousness of this issue."

"Can you make a list of the items?"

"A list?"

"A detailed inventory of what was in the garage."

"Er, well . . ."

"Just look at your garage—you can park both of your cars in there! And you haven't even looked in your garden shed yet."

"You went into my shed?"

"Sure. Originally I quoted your wife seventy-five dollars for the garage, but I got done so fast that I threw in the shed for free."

"What are we going to do with all those piles of garbage?" Mr. Hedrick asked. "You can't just leave them; trash day is a whole week away and all that junk downgrades the value of the neighborhood."

"For an extra forty dollars, I can take care of that."

He gave me the money. I pulled a broken sled out of the pile and started loading. I dragged the sled two blocks over to the alley behind the motorcycle repair garage, which is full of industrial-sized Dumpsters.

Then I jogged back to Mrs. Middlebrook's house and pocketed another forty dollars for taking her stuff to the Dumpsters.

It was still only late afternoon. By dusk, I had gutted two more garages, and the Dumpsters in the alley were overflowing.

Not only was I a really hard worker, but I had psychological insight into people; my talents were more about getting them to let go of stuff than just cleaning their garages. What can I say?

I'm a people person.

I wished Tina lived closer to my neighborhood so that I could work my way to her house, one filthy garage at a time.

Then I took a whiff of myself and was glad she lived on the other side of town.

But I'd made $475 in one day. Unbelievable!

That was more money than I'd ever had at one time. I'd have to take a few bucks off the bottom line for work gloves, and the hydrogen peroxide and anti-infection ointment I'd need to treat the raccoon potty itch, but still, I had launched another business.

This getting rich thing was turning out to be a snap.

The Successful Person Knows When to Revise and Expand His Plans Quickly

later on Saturday, after I'd scrubbed my filthy skin raw to remove the grit of a thousand cumulative years of dust and crud, we had a family dinner.

Luckily, my parents had both been working really hard and it was a fast dinner of turkey tetrazzini from the freezer. Afterwards they went to "read." That means doze on the couch. I waited until Mom's head fell back and Dad started snoring before I ran over to the college campus to make sure the game at the dorm was going well and collect my fee. Then I ran to the store and then to Auntie

Buzz's office to take Daniel's hockey team grape soda and tortilla chips and collect my fee. "Don't make crumbs or spill," I told them. But I still made a mental note to come by early the next morning to clean up after them.

I worked fast and was home in time to meet JonPaul on the driveway; he was coming over to watch movies, like he does every Saturday night. I peeked into the living room on our way to the kitchen. My mother was actually reading and my father was thumb-typing on his phone, but neither had noticed I was gone during their little catnaps. I was hardworking *and* stealthy. Awesome.

I whipped up a batch of that dry breakfast cereal/melted chocolate/melted peanut butter/melted butter/dash of vanilla/tons of powdered sugar stuff we like so well.

"Man," JonPaul said, "there is nothing as wonderful in the world as late-night munchies."

That reminded me of the lame lemonade stand idea that I'd set aside. As JonPaul snarfed, I thought back to Goober's dorm room earlier that evening when I'd dropped off the tortilla chips and soda and gone over the rules *again*. Then I remembered watching my mother and father drink coffee and come to life every morning of my life before they leave for work. I also took note of the fact that I'm something of a night owl and can get by on less sleep than the average fourteen-year-old.

"I've got it!" I jumped up and started pacing. The best ideas come when you pace. I don't know why. I guess people with brains like mine need activity to jump-start creativity. Or else I was on a sugar high.

"Got what?" JonPaul looked at me warily.

"Our new venture. You, me and Sam. Catering."

"Huh?"

"College students are pretty much fried and dragging at around ten-thirty, eleven at night after a full day of classes and then studying all evening. Right?"

He nodded.

"Okay, so we rig up a coffeepot and throw together a few batches of cookies and brownies. We borrow Markie's wagon and drag it around campus at night selling munchies."

"You think that'll work?"

"Why wouldn't it? They're hungry, craving sugar, but too lazy or busy to go get stuff. We bring the supply to the demand and *bingo!* We'll clean up."

"You're amazing, Kev. The way you . . ."

"Thanks, JonPaul, it's a gift."

"How are we going to pay for the cookie and coffee stuff?"

"I made money today cleaning garages. Spending my own money worked for the poker game; I made back my investment the first night."

We figured that Sunday, tomorrow, would be the ideal day to start. The students would have had Friday and Saturday nights to cut loose but would be facing Monday morning and the start of a new class week. We guessed that Sundays were prime cram nights on campus.

First thing in the morning, I bribed Sarah to take me to the huge warehouse store, where I bought fifty-pound bags of flour and of sugar, small-car-sized boxes of chocolate chips, and plastic bins for the cookies. I made careful note of the ten dollars I paid her. The cost of doing business. I'd have to set up a bookkeeping program on the computer.

JonPaul and Sam were waiting in the kitchen when we got home. Not only did Sam arrive wearing an apron, but she went right to work setting up stations of ingredients to form an assembly line and speed up the process.

My dad, getting coffee on the way to the living room to read the Sunday papers with my mom, raised an eyebrow.

"I'm starting a business!" I gestured to all the stuff on the counters. "All by myself. Well, except for JonPaul and Sam." Dad had probably noticed them standing next to the oven.

"Looks like a lot of work," Dad said.

"Nah. I've got everything covered. Nothing to worry about," I told him.

He looked doubtful but finally nodded. "I'm going to take your mother a cup of coffee and tell her there's a perfect example of capitalism in action in her kitchen."

"She'll be pretty happy about that, I bet," I told him.

"She'll be happy if you clean up when you're done."

I waved off his concerns. But JonPaul looked worried.

"How are we going to do this in one day, just the three of us?" he asked.

"Time-management skills, JonPaul, multitasking. Doing one thing at a time is for losers. Professionals know how to maximize their time. We can even do our homework while the cookies and brownies bake. I stayed up late last night thinking this through—I've got everything covered."

"We don't have any eggs," Sam piped up just then, "and the recipe you got off the Internet for these cookies says we need eggs."

Eggs. I'd forgotten eggs. And butter.

I made my second trip to the store. Sarah sighed a lot in the car like I'd taken her away from something more important than long conversations on the phone with her new boyfriend, Doug. After we picked up the butter and eggs and dropped them off with Sam and JonPaul, I had her drive me to church, where I borrowed a coffee urn from the basement social hall. The last time our family had helped with a church party, I'd noticed that one of the urns was in a back closet because it had a crack near the spigot.

But that's what duct tape is for.

When I returned home, Sam and JonPaul had made up a bunch of batches of cookie dough and had them ready to be dumped in spoon-sized blobs on cookie sheets and put in the oven. Except that we didn't have nearly enough baking sheets.

Good thing I'd gotten the coffeepot when I did, because it reminded me that we couldn't sell piping-hot coffee to bare, cupped hands—we needed actual cups. Ooh, and napkins. Rats, this was turning out to be complicated.

JonPaul and Sam measured coffee while I headed out again, on my third trip to the wholesale store for cookie sheets, paper napkins and coffee cups. And milk. Sarah rolled her eyes at me, but I don't know why she was annoyed. She could talk to Doug just as easily waiting for me in the parking lot as lying in her bedroom, and at least this way, she was helping me start an empire. Some people only think of themselves.

The guard checking membership cards at the

warehouse store's door did a double take when he saw me arrive for the third time in a day. Then he followed me around the store.

As if I'm gonna shove a 250-pack of triple-A batteries down my shorts or stick the 7,000-piece-of-gum box under my shirt. Unless you're a kangaroo or a minivan, shoplifting isn't really an option at the wholesale store.

Finally, we had all the supplies and the house was filling with the smell of melting chocolate. Jon-Paul and Sam sat at the counter doing homework while I created a master list of supplies so that the next baking day would go more smoothly. Then I set up accounting systems for the poker games, Sarah's beauty salon, my cleaning service and the munchies runs. Wow. I wondered what people did when they had more money than they knew what to do with. I couldn't wait to find out.

"You know," JonPaul said, looking at my outfit as we were getting ready to leave the house that night, "blue and orange aren't really your colors."

"I know that. Who in their right mind would wear an orange stocking cap and a shiny blue— what is this material, anyway?—warm-up jacket?

But these are the college colors and we're going to show school spirit. And I really do appreciate your efforts on behalf of this marketing and promotion idea."

"I had to think long and hard before I painted 'Go Huskies' on my face! This stuff will come off, right? It's not toxic, is it? Because lead can cause liver failure and kidney disease and brain damage in young people, you know, and I could develop respiratory distress. If I do, you know, start to gasp and turn blue, well, *more* blue, I guess, underneath the face paint, can I count on you to revive me with assisted breathing until the paramedics arrive?"

"Uh-huh."

"You don't sound committed."

"Believe me, JonPaul, I'm committed to the idea of not having you keel over dead in the middle of a transaction. Bad for business."

Sam had to go home for dinner, so it was just me and JonPaul hitting the bricks with Markie's wagon and a dream. Mom and Auntie Buzz were going to a book club meeting, so they'd given Sam a ride home. I'd handed them each a cookie as thanks.

"Next time, save me a blob of the raw dough,"

Auntie Buzz said. "The baked stuff isn't half as good."

I nodded, but my mother shook her head. "Salmonella, Buzz."

I was glad she hadn't seen how many fingerfuls of dough I'd eaten all day. You know, to keep my energy up. Nothing like melted butter and two kinds of sugar, plus chocolate chips, to give a guy a boost. Plus, I'm sure salmawhatsit only affects older people.

The hope was that JonPaul and I would do modest sales the first time out, spread the word and build a client base over time.

We were swarmed from the start. Hands were grabbing for coffee and cookies and thrusting crumpled bills and fistfuls of change at us.

We only managed to get to one dorm before we ran out of everything. And the college had four dorms on the side of campus closest to my house.

Hmm. I was going to have to think bigger. Nightly campus runs. Skip Fridays and Saturdays, though.

I was sitting in the kitchen the next day after

school while that night's brownies baked, realizing that Markie's wagon had already become obsolete. I needed more efficient transportation.

I was thinking about my options when my dad came home from a business game at the golf course midfume.

My dad has a habit of starting in talking to people like they've heard the first part of a conversation that actually happened somewhere else, so I didn't understand what he was going on about. I just nodded along until I finally figured out that he was furious about the defective golf cart he'd rented.

"It doesn't go over three-point-eight miles an hour, I couldn't put it in reverse and the steering wheel stuck if I tried to turn left. I could only make right-hand turns! We abandoned it on the sixth hole and called the clubhouse to complain."

A golf cart. Really nothing more than a minicar.

And a minicar is really nothing more than a microvan.

Perfect.

"What happened to the cart then, Dad?" I asked, very calm even though I was so excited I could have hovercrafted myself over to the golf course.

"They towed that fragmented pile of motorized rubble to the maintenance shed for repairs. They should shoot it between the eyes, that's what they should do."

Dad's phone rang. He ruffled my hair on his way to his home office.

I dug through his golf bag and found the map to the course that was printed on the back of the scorecard. One reason we live where we do is that we can walk to the course.

I studied the map and found the garage. Then I traced a route of right-hand turns (and, of course, forward gear) only, back to my house. I'd go for the cart as soon as darkness fell. When I got back, Jon-Paul and Sam would be waiting to load it with our baked goods.

I took four of the most perfect-looking cookies and two corner pieces of the brownies and wrapped them carefully in plastic wrap. I'd offer them to Tina the next day at lunch and casually mention my new business. Girls like guys who can cook and bake. I'd read that it makes us seem sensitive and thoughtful or something. Finally! I'd come up with a way to make her aware of how hard I was working to be the ultimate boyfriend. There's no way a girl is going to pass up the chance to date a guy who bakes from scratch. If I was a girl, I'd date a guy like me, and I have very high standards.

8

The Successful Person Knows He Is a Force for Good in the Universe

I nodded off in homeroom Tuesday morning. There's something about daily announcements that puts me to sleep. Plus, I'd worked really hard the past two nights. The income stream was good, I thought, but the output of effort was bad. I was going to need another variable to even things out in my getting-rich plan.

I was going to need another business partner. Preferably one who already had a blossoming sideline and could benefit from my skills to make it into something much more impressive, like I'd done with Sarah.

I glanced around homeroom. Any likely candidates?

Sometimes the last thing you'd ever think of is the first thing you should consider. The difference between being smart and being really smart is looking at things in a way no one would ever expect.

"I need Katie Knowles," I told JonPaul in the hallway on the way to first period. "She's the next piece of the puzzle."

"She's still not speaking to you after the way you lied to her about the social studies project a couple weeks ago," he said, looking at me like I was crazy. "She doesn't like you."

"No, that's not it. She loathes and despises me."

"Yeah, well, then, how do you figure she's going to work for you?"

"While it's true that she looks at me like she's wishing my internal organs would fall out of my body and land with a wet *thwack* on the ground, I think she's just waiting for me to make the first move."

"And what move would that be?"

"A job offer."

"You're going to offer a job to a girl who pretends you don't exist and believes you're not worth talking to?"

"I don't need her to talk to me. We can communicate through notes—I told you about those abstract thingies she wrote for the social studies project, right? She'll probably appreciate correspondence rather than conversation."

"Why would she bother?"

"Simple. I can give her what she wants most in the world: malleable minds to sculpt."

"How does that work?"

"You know she tutors, right?"

"Yeah."

"Dude. She's doing that for *free*."

His silence proved that he was as horrified by that as I was.

"I know. Wrong, so wrong, so very wrong, isn't it? Giving away a valuable service like that for nothing. It's unnatural."

"How do you fit in?"

"As the, uh, purveyor of, um, managerial services."

"Huh?"

"I am exactly the right person to help her make

more of her little tutoring gig by giving it some professional flair."

"I'm pretty sure she won't see it like that."

"I'm going to talk to her about it today."

"I thought you were going to write."

"I can't propose a partnership other than face to face."

"I hope she doesn't laugh in your face. Or slap it. Or—"

"Yeah, I get the picture. But I'm not worried. I'm a very persuasive guy, and I only need to say a few words to convince her."

"If you say so." JonPaul was doubtful. A lesser guy than me would have held his lack of faith in me against him, but I just felt sorry that he didn't believe in me as much as I did. Because believing in someone like me is a great thing. He'll see. He just needs time.

At lunch, I went right over to Katie's table. She looked up.

"Kevin."

Funny how one girl saying one word can make your blood run cold.

I flashed what I hoped was a dazzling smile at

her. "Katie. Good to see you. You look great. How're you doing these days?"

"What do you want?"

"I like a person who cuts to the chase. Clearly, small talk is wasted on someone of your intelligence. I'll get right to the point: I have a business proposition for you."

"What? I do the work and you get the credit? Like the last time?"

"I see you're still upset about our . . . misunderstanding. I'd hoped you'd put that behind you."

"People don't so much put that kind of thing behind them as learn from their mistakes. And what I learned is to stay far away from you."

"Point taken. But hear me out, because I have an idea that is going to appeal to you both academically and financially."

She didn't laugh or hit me or run away or lean over and puke on my shoes, so I quickly explained.

"For a small fee, a teeny, tiny percentage of your earnings, I will help you transform your informal tutoring situation into a structured educational enrichment provider."

I was using my best and most impressive vocab;

I thought I sounded pretty good—I just hoped I was making sense. So much of this business jargon sounds stupid to me.

"You think I'm going to pay you to come in and meddle with my tutoring? That I don't even charge for in the first place because that would be shallow and unfair and then I couldn't use the sessions as my service hour requirements anymore?"

"At the current time, you have no profits, but I could change that. And there's nothing wrong with being compensated for your services. Besides, people value what they pay for. You'll be making yourself look more professional and worthwhile if you start charging. And you'll get more work out of your students."

She didn't say anything for a second, but I knew she was tempted.

"What do you have in mind? Precisely?"

"We sit down with the yearbook and figure out which kids are vulnerable in a GPA kind of way and then we send letters to their parents offering your services and spelling out what you charge. Given your reputation as a brainiac, we sit back and wait for the flood of job offers."

"It's that easy?"

"Sure. Doesn't it *sound* easy?"

"It sounds smart. That's not like you."

Ouch.

"Look, I've got this computer system that I set up to keep track of your appointments. I'll do all the scheduling for you. You won't have to do a thing but teach. Which you're doing anyway. And collect the money. Which you're not doing."

She looked torn.

"Are you in?"

She bit her lip.

"This will look *ah-may-zing* on your college applications."

"I'm in."

"Good. Meet me here after school and we'll walk back to my house together and get started on the letters."

She laughed. Snorted, really.

"Right. Like I'm not going to have finished and polished final drafts by the end of the school day."

I may not like Katie Knowles. But I absolutely love Katie Knowles. I wish I could bottle her crazed perfectionism. She's got all the right stuff for a corporate whiz kid.

I noticed that Tina was sitting a table over and had probably noticed me talking to Katie. Perfect! Guys always look more attractive to girls when they're talking to other girls. I heard Sarah say that once. I am a genius even when I'm not working at it.

The Successful Person Is Not Afraid to Admit That He Is Easily Intimidated by a Show of Force

I was walking home after school that afternoon, planning: It was my babysitting day, so I'd pick Markie up at his house, take him to my place and start baking before JonPaul and Sam showed up. Maybe that way I'd have time to make a few extra batches and we could hit another dorm that evening.

"Dutchdeefuddy. I'm learning how to spell," Markie told me as we cut through the yard between our houses. *"C-A-T. Cat. D-O-G. Dog. B-A-R-F. Barf. F-A-R-T. Fart."*

"How'd you learn to do that, Markie?"

"Mommy gave me a toy where I press the letters and the voice inside tells me if I got the word right. *T-O-O-T. Toot. B-U-R-P. Burp.*"

"Very impressive. Here's another one: *B-A-K-E. Bake.* You're going to help make cookies today."

"Can I lick the bowl and shout *'BAM!'* really loud?"

"Yeah, sure, just don't go near the oven. And don't touch anything sharp."

"*O-K. Okay.*"

As soon as we got to my house, I gave Markie the flour sifter and tied an apron around him. He was making a mess, but at least he wasn't going to slow me down. I had my baking schedule timed to the second.

I'd put the first batch in the oven when my mother pulled a boxed spaghetti dinner from the freezer and put it in the microwave. My family had learned to work around needing the kitchen while JonPaul and Sam and I baked every day. Mom clapped when Markie spelled *M-O-M*, and she pretended not to see the pile of sifted flour on the floor while she waited for her food to nuke.

"Your father has a business dinner, Sarah and

Auntie Buzz are going out to eat and catch a movie, and Daniel is at a team banquet. We won't bother you in the kitchen today. But"—she hesitated, choosing her words carefully—"we're wondering how much longer we're going to be eating sandwiches in the family room every evening."

"Yeah, well, see, the thing is that I'm really on to something here. Everything is going so well: Sarah is booked back to back with clients, I just talked Katie into letting me manage her tutoring job, I have six garages scheduled for this weekend, Jon-Paul and I are doing dorm runs five nights a week, and the poker ga—"

"Poker?" Even though I'd tried to bite off the last few words, my mother caught them. And she didn't look happy about my success or proud of my efforts.

"I'm keeping up with my homework." I tried to show her the bright side.

"Don't change the subject. What's this about poker?"

"I'm not lying anymore," I reminded her.

Before she could continue pursuing the poker game issue, her cell phone chimed. She looked at the screen, frowned and said, "Work," as she headed off to her desk in the family room. "But we will definitely talk about this poker situation later."

I took her dinner out of the microwave and gave it to Markie. There. Now I didn't have to worry about feeding him later.

I sighed and turned back to my pan of cookies, peering at the temperature knob because the oven seemed to be running a little hot; this last batch had looked a tad overdone.

"B-I-G. Big," Markie spelled.

"What's big?" I asked.

"H-I-M. Him," Markie said. I looked up and saw that he was pointing toward the back door.

Where a couple of very big, very solid guys about nineteen or twenty years old stood. "Who the heck are you?" I asked.

"I'm Dash's older brother, Wally."

Oh no.

Despite my coaching at the game the night before, Dash had still been trying to read the other players' faces and had bet according to what he thought their hands were rather than what his cards were. He'd lost. A lot.

"And I'm Joe, the resident advisor on Goober's dorm floor."

"We work together at the martial arts school," Wally said. "I was telling him how my kid brother is losing his butt in a poker game and he mentioned that these five drips on his floor do nothing but play poker. They've been cutting class trying to get good."

"What a coincidence that you two would know each other," I said, trying to put a positive spin on what was feeling potentially very negative.

"You're the house, right?" Joe asked.

I nodded and felt an ugly clench in my gut, in the place that usually feels really bad just before I spend a whole lot of time in the bathroom. Funny how terror and the runs have so much in common.

"And taking a profit per hand?" Wally asked.

Per hand? Shut. The. Front. Door.

That never crossed my mind. Why hadn't I figured that out on my own?

"Um, well, no . . . see, the games—"

"How many poker games are you running?" Joe squinted at me.

"Three."

"You're taking money from three different sets of idiots who don't know the first thing about cards?" Wally pounded one fist into the other. I hoped it was a nervous tic and not the sign of things to come.

"No! It's only Dash who doesn't have a clu . . ." I trailed off when I saw Wally frown.

"The way I see it," Wally said, "Dash either starts winning—which, let's face it, is not about to happen, because that kid can't play poker—or the game ends so he can't get into any more trouble."

"No, wait," Joe said, "I think *all* the games end so that *you* don't get in any more trouble."

"I'm not in any trouble."

"Yeah. You are." Joe looked down at me.

"You're just too dumb to have figured that out yet." Wally did the pounding fist thing again.

"I never thought anyone would get upset."

"No one's upset. Yet." Joe nodded.

"Stop the games and everything's fine," Wally said. "Dash will stop losing money and pay me back what I've lent him."

"If you don't stop the games," Joe said as he and Wally headed out the kitchen door, "we'll have to come back, and we might not be so nice."

"*N-I-C-E. Nice.*" Markie waved goodbye to Wally and Joe from the table, where he'd been eating spaghetti and watching me get threatened.

'Vorces and bankruptcy and now intimidation. Man, for a four-year-old, Markie was really racking up the life experiences.

Good thing Tina and I weren't officially going out together yet. No one wants a boyfriend who gets caught up in seedy stuff like this.

The timer dinged and I took the cookies out of the oven. This batch was perfect, and my mood lifted a little. The poker games might be over, but my other ideas were still okay. Every business was bound to go over a few bumps. I was just getting mine out of the way in the beginning so that I could look forward to smooth sailing from here on in.

JonPaul and Sam showed up and, as JonPaul made the coffee and Sam packed the cookies in plastic containers, I told them about the end of my poker games.

"Thatwasfast," Sam said. "You'donlyhadthem foraweek."

"Maybe I was too diversified," I said. "You know, I had too much going on and my attention was spread too thin. This is probably for the best. Now I can focus on what really matters."

"P-O-O-P. Poop," Markie sang out.

You got that right, kid.

10

The Successful Person Knows That the Bigger the Problem Seems, the More Extraordinary the Solution Will Be

I shook off the disappointment of being forced to shut down the games. Guys who want to be successful have to learn to live with setbacks. I started making phone calls to the players letting them know that the game was over, while Sam made a spelling list for Markie, and JonPaul went to get the cart from the golf course.

Goober thought my experience with Joe was subversive and cool. I was mostly surprised he knew the meaning of the word *subversive*, considering he still couldn't play a hand of poker without referring to a crib sheet. Truthfully, Goober and his buddies were probably glad the stress of counting and keeping colors straight was over.

Wheels and the other guys were just as happy to go back to playing for points in the lunchroom. Much safer.

I was still kind of hoping to be able to keep the hockey team's game up and running. But then Auntie Buzz popped into the office to pick up a color wheel, saw the cards and the chips and the mess that I hadn't cleaned up yet and went all psycho on me in a text. I read it in the golf cart while JonPaul and Sam sold our munchies.

"U R gambling in my office! Ill talk 2 ur mthr 18er! Stop rite now!"

Saturday morning, I was busy dragging sleds full of junk from various garages in my neighborhood to the Dumpsters in the alley.

I was also thinking that my neighbors were lazy or they all suffered from a hoarding complex, because I must have single-handedly rid our subdivision of several tons of worthless stuff.

As I was chucking out an ancient space heater, some fondue forks and a stack of old magazines (nothing good—I checked), a huge guy jumped out from behind a tow truck parked in the alley.

"You! Stop putting garbage in that Dumpster!"

"Who are you?"

"I'm the manager of the motorcycle repair garage, and I've been sitting out here for three hours waiting to see who's been dumping all the crap in my Dumpsters."

Your Dumpsters? Oh.

"Why?"

"You've been overloading them! I'm getting charged a fortune in extra fees and penalties by the garbage company for going over our contracted trash allotment."

"You mean hauling away garbage isn't free?"

"No way, kid! Nothing is free."

I should have known that.

Long story short: I was now responsible for an insane garbage bill. The guy gave me a card with the garbage company manager's phone number so that I could make arrangements.

Then he watched me while I climbed into the

Dumpster and removed the junk I'd deposited, replacing it on my sled.

I dragged the sled back to my house and stuck it in the back of our garage. Maybe this was part of the reason all those garages had gotten so cluttered in the first place: it's not easy to dump your stuff.

I didn't have to be a rocket scientist to spot the downward momentum. I'd been forced to give up my poker games, my clutter-removal days were probably over and I had to call Amalgamated Waste Management to get on a payment plan.

I talked to a nice guy in accounts receivable who gave me the option of paying the bill or working it off. Work is, all evidence to the contrary lately, a good thing. So is hanging on to the money I'd made. We made a deal: I'd come down to the offices twice a week for a while until I'd gotten square with them. I didn't even ask what I'd be doing. It was garbage. It couldn't be good.

I cheered myself up by remembering that all great men took pride in starting at the bottom. This would build character. And make a great story when someone eventually wrote my biography.

It's looking on the bright side that sets the successes apart from the failures.

Good thing I didn't have the poker games to worry about anymore, because otherwise I wouldn't have had the time to work for Amalgamated Waste Management.

11

The Successful Person Is Frequently Misunderstood and Unappreciated

The next evening, everything was going fine, or what passed for fine in a collapsing universe. JonPaul, Sam and I were preparing for a busy night of sales.

We started putt-putt-putting along from dorm to dorm, making only right-hand turns at no greater speed than 3.8 miles an hour.

Until a gung-ho security guard zipped up on a Segway.

"You! Stop in the name of the law!"

We stopped.

"I'm ordering you to cease and desist all movement."

The three of us didn't move except to look at each other and roll our eyes.

"Refrain from further mobility in the name of the college."

Well, now, this was getting interesting.

"By the powers vested in me by Carl, the chief of security, I hereby place you under arrest."

Oh, come on now. "Arrested" by a college security guard. Who was riding a Segway and didn't even have a Taser or a nightstick. All she had was a radio. And what was she going to do, turn up the volume really loud, talk at the same time someone was speaking to her and static us into submission?

"I've been watching you. You filth peddlers and destroyers of fine young minds! You should be ashamed of yourselves!"

Crazy lady on a nifty scooter say what?

"Whatareyoutalkingabout?" Sam asked.

JonPaul did his best impression of a tree stump: said nothing. Sat motionless. I'd like to think it was because he knew that letting me handle things was the best course of action.

"Illegal substances."

"The sugar, butter, chocolate or caffeine?" I asked her.

"Don't get smart with me! I've read all about people like you. Drug pusher!"

I was flummoxed. "You think we're selling drugs from the back of a golf cart?"

"You have the ideal setup, and those baby faces of yours are the perfect cover."

"We're fourteen years old. We're selling cookies and coffee."

"And besides," Sam piped up, "I promised my mother I wouldneveringestpharmaceuticallyimpure substances, much less *sell* them."

"You sound sincere." The guard was disappointed.

"We are."

She finally noticed that we were not on foot.

"Do you have a license to drive that thing?"

"It's a golf cart; I didn't think I needed a license," I said from behind the wheel.

"You need a license to operate a motorized vehicle. That's the law."

I tried to explain how our crappy little golf cart

really could hardly be considered a motorized vehicle. "It doesn't go over three-point-eight miles an hour, we can't put it in reverse and the steering wheel sticks if you try to turn left, so we can only make right-hand turns."

"Where'd you get it?"

"The golf course near my house. They, um, had retired it."

Her eyes widened.

"Grand theft auto," she whispered slowly, and I saw her tremble slightly.

"I wouldn't go that far. I return the cart every night, I only borrow it when it's dark and no one's playing golf anyway and I refill the tank before leaving. It doesn't even have an odometer."

"Well, when you put it that way, I guess you haven't really broken any laws . . ." She trailed off sadly.

Her dreams were tanking. She made one last stand.

"You have *got* to be in violation of something. Maybe some kind of food-handling codes? I can't believe you haven't trashed health department stand— OH, SWEET FDA REGULATIONS! You're not wearing plastic gloves! You are touching the food with your bare hands."

"You think that's a problem?"

"Only if you don't want to spread salmonella, botulism, and possibly Legionnaires' disease."

"Oh. I'm sure that's not an issue." I tried to remember if I'd always washed my hands. The odds were not in my favor.

I looked back at the remaining cookies and brownies in the plastic containers on the back of the golf cart.

"They'recrawlingwithfoodcooties!" the security guard said, sounding an awful lot like Sam, who wasn't saying anything.

How come JonPaul, the king of germs, hadn't thought about this? I glanced over at him, annoyed. The guy has one obsession in life and he forgets it when it could have helped us out. Geez.

"How'd you get into this line of work, anyway?" I asked the guard. Everyone's favorite subject is themselves, and if you turn the focus on them, they usually forget where the conversation was headed.

"I need my days free so that I can pursue my real passion," she said, smiling. "I bead. I make jewelry by hand."

"Big future in that?"

"It's a nice sideline. I want to save up enough so that I can invest in my business and go full-time."

"What kind of clasps do you use?" JonPaul finally spoke up.

"You know about beading?" She beamed. I tried not to tip over in surprise. JonPaul beads? Just when you think you know a guy, he goes and pulls something like this. Sam's influence? She was smiling, not looking surprised by Bead Boy at all.

We made introductions. The guard's name was Renee. And then JonPaul and Sam exchanged contact info with Renee so they could get together and make jewelry.

As they talked to Renee, I studied JonPaul. He hadn't just lost three businesses in two days, and he actually had a real girlfriend instead of just plotting ways to impress someone like I did with Tina, and he seemed to have picked up a new hobby that he enjoyed.

Yeah, I know that even the best businesspeople

feel down from time to time, but I was starting to wonder: did I really have what it took to get filthy, stinking rich at age fourteen? Nothing had gone like I thought it was going to.

Nah, I just needed a good night's sleep. I'd feel better in the morning and would come up with a new plan, a better plan, a foolproof plan.

JonPaul, Sam and I putt-putt-putted back home—but only after we emptied the unsold cookies into a trash can on campus.

They were so jazzed about beading with Renee that they didn't seem to realize we didn't have a munchie business anymore. Or maybe they did and they were glad. Neither of them had been as set on getting rich as I was. They'd been working for minimum wage, but I had been pursuing my calling in life. There's a big difference between working for a paycheck and striving toward a dream, I realized.

The Successful Person Knows His Limits

I didn't want to get out of bed the next morning. I lay there and thought.

Okay, I was down, but I still had the management positions with Sarah and Katie and a notebook full of ideas. Still . . . I was getting a little panicky. I just had to get some new ideas hatched.

I texted JonPaul and Sam: "Emergency meeting @ HQ l8er 2day. Discuss team status."

After school, I was pacing back and forth, or what passes for pacing in a broom closet, waiting for them to arrive.

My hopes and dreams and plans for the rest of my life hinged on the prompt rebuilding of Kevin L. Spencer Corporation. V.2.0, of course.

They finally arrived, and I pulled them into the office.

I struggled to shut the closet door, then remembered that the frame was warped and the door didn't shut all the way, which was why Buzz didn't use the space.

A pep talk was in order. I had to instill confidence in them. They were depending on me. I had to set a good example. Everyone would naturally look to me for guidance.

JonPaul leaned against the wall, picking raisins out of an oatmeal cookie. Sam was nowhere to be seen.

"Where's Sam?"

"Down here," came a tiny voice.

I crouched down and saw her hunched under the desk with a thermos balanced on one knee and a plastic bag of grapes in her hand.

"Look, Sam, just because we're faced with unexpected challenges is no reason to hide under the desk."

"She's not hiding," JonPaul pointed out. "There's no room with the door even half shut."

"Oh. Well. I have a plan for reorganization and refocus," I announced in a voice that sounded too high and nervous to be mine. I cleared my throat and took a deep breath. "Things haven't quite worked out, so I'm advancing in a new direction. Hence my New Plan. My Better Plan."

"Sam and I have been talking, and we think your goose is cooked," Jon Paul said. He might have sounded mean, but he's not like that. Still, that's not the kind of thing a guy wants to hear.

"No, wait, don't make up your mind too fast," I told him. "Hear me out."

"Buddy, I want to be supportive, I really do, but your whole moneymaking thing is a bad idea."

"I just need to reevaluate."

"Look, Kev: I hate to let you down, but Sam and I aren't going to be able to keep working for you."

This blatant act of insubordination would go in their personnel records! I hoped they knew we'd be discussing *this* at their annual reviews.

"I'mreallysorryKev," came Sam's voice from under the desk, "but . . . umph, um, you guys? Some help, please, I'mkindofwedgedunderneathhereand Ican'tfeelmylegs."

We helped Sam crawl out from under the desk and held her up until the pins and needles went away.

"We're just not cut out to work with a mogul," JonPaul said.

"Wetalkedaboutitandweagreedthatwe'renotright foryourcompany," Sam said. "It's not you, it's us."

Wow. I'd never even had a girlfriend and yet I was getting dumped with the oldest line in the book.

I couldn't think of a single reason they should stay with me. That wasn't like me; usually I can come up with twenty good reasons to do anything.

Sam hugged me and JonPaul punched my arm before they left. I knew they cared. But I crossed them off my list of people I was talking to.

Sure, they weren't supposed to have my vision or bravery, but they were supposed to be loyal and supportive. They were supposed to follow my lead for a little longer than a week.

I slunk home to go back to bed and sleep the rest of the week away.

Instead, I found Katie Knowles, Sarah and her boyfriend, Doug, at the kitchen table.

"I'm terminating our working agreement, Kev," Sarah said. "Doug here is going to handle the bookings. He charges less than you do. And the whole thing about me paying you part of my earnings because you suggested I charge a fee is ridiculous. I've paid you enough already."

When I opened my mouth, she held up a hand. "You're not in a position to argue. Be smart enough to know when you're ahead and let it go." Doug nodded and patted the laptop in front of him.

I looked over at Katie. "You too?"

She nodded. Guess she still wasn't speaking to me.

"Doug," Sarah informed me, "is also going to be doing Katie's tutoring appointments, since he knows the computer system already."

They got up and left the kitchen. I heard them go into our/Sarah's bathroom. Sarah was saying, "Let me show you how to highlight your cheekbones."

Well, I should consider myself lucky to be rid of them. I was better off. No dead weight. Now I could launch the Kevin L. Spencer Corporation without any friends and family holding me back.

Things looked bad. But I knew I would have to find a way to make this my finest hour. Somehow, I'd have to dig down deep to rally in an admirable manner that spoke to the quality of my character and the unquenchable strength of my dream. Or however businesspeople put it.

And then they'd all be sorry they'd turned on me.

Great men are never appreciated in their time. I'd read that, but now I was living it. It sounded kind of cool, but it felt kind of crummy.

13

The Successful Person is Steadfast in the Face of Disaster, Can Cope with Multiple Crises at One Time and Learns from His Mistakes

I went back to my room and looked at my piles of military history and business books on the floor for new ideas about what to do next.

Nah. I needed something stronger than a book. I needed my parents.

I found them reading in the family room.

"Hey, Kev, how are you?" Mom asked.

"Abysmal."

"When last I checked, 'fine' was still the standard answer," Dad joked.

"Not in my world."

I told them what had happened: how all my dreams had crashed, how I never wanted to talk to JonPaul and Sam and Sarah and Katie again and how the feeling was probably mutual.

"I'll give you this much: when you mess up, it's always in a big way," Dad said.

"Everything sounded like such a good idea."

"Everything always does, hon." Mom smiled.

"Why do things like this happen to me?"

My mother and father looked at each other. Each clearly hoping the other had a good answer.

"Forget I asked. I know why things like this always happen to me: I make them happen."

"Well, son, you're never boring. No one could ever say you were a dull person. And that counts for a lot."

"How do I turn things around?"

My mother and father looked at each other. Each clearly hoping I'd come up with the answer myself.

I sighed.

"I'm going to have to apologize again, aren't I?

Go around undoing the bad things and making things right again, aren't I?"

"Well, yes," Dad said. "But look at the bright side: you've done it before and it's bound to be easier the second time around."

"There's no other way?"

"Not that I know of," Mom said.

"I was afraid you'd say that."

"Getting out of trouble is a whole lot more of a hassle than staying out of trouble," Dad said.

"I'm starting to figure that out."

I wasn't ready to make the amends tour again just yet, and I was half-hoping there was an easier way out of this predicament. So I did what had seemed to make sense the last time I'd been in a jam: I went to see Markie.

He'd take my mind off things. He always does. There's no way Markie has any idea what's going on, and he won't remind me what a lousy, greedy person I've been lately.

"Hey, Dutchdeefuddy," Markie called from his swing set as I walked to his backyard. *"S-O-R-R-Y. Sorry."*

I stopped dead in my tracks.

"What did you just say?"

"Wanna play Sorry?"

"You're kidding me, right?"

"No, Sorry is a great game. And it's easy, too."

We'll see about that, Markie, we'll just see about that.

The Successful Person is Capable of Moving On from Multifaceted Calamities with Humor and Grace

I apologized to Sam and JonPaul for taking advantage of them with the munchies situation. They were really happy when I busted out the money we'd earned and split it into three even shares rather than paying them hourly wages. It was only fair: we were a team.

I took freshly baked cookies and brownies to the manager of the motorcycle repair garage to apologize for having loaded his Dumpsters.

On the way home, I noticed a little bakery downtown that had just opened and didn't seem to be doing very well. I made an appointment to see the manager and told her about my former campus munchies business. I watched her eyes light up. Then I introduced her to Goober, and she hired him to do the food runs. He needed a job after all that money he'd lost playing poker.

I was surprised, but . . . I guess the blind pursuit of money and power really is bad for a person. Who knew?

Well, everyone, I guess, except me.

Despite the fact that all my ideas turned into poo on a stick, everyone around me farts gold dust these days.

Sarah's not mad at me, even though I suspect she still thinks I took too much credit for her new business, which, I might point out, landed her a part-time job at the hair salon.

Katie's not talking to me, but that's nothing new. She does nod at me in the hall. I take that as progress. And she's going to have to hire some tutors to handle all her students.

I learned from Sarah and Katie that it's always better to make money with your own ideas than to sponge off others.

JonPaul and Sam and Renee the security guard

are jewelry-making partners. They're talking about going to art fairs this summer to sell their goods. JonPaul and Renee are the creative side, and Sam takes care of supplies and inventory and their website.

They taught me that successful people stick to what they're good at and what makes them happy.

Daniel, that sly dog, took what used to be poker time and started giving skating lessons to little kids. The team worked out a deal with the rink; they teach the itty-bitty skater classes in exchange for discounted ice time. Daniel says the team's reactions have gotten really sharp because of how fast they've had to learn to stop and catch the toppled toddlers.

They taught me that hobbies and jobs can have some overlap; and that maybe, if you like what you do, you don't need to blow off steam.

No one has even bothered to thank me for starting them out. I'm glad I don't have their karma, because that kind of ingratitude is going to come home to roost someday. Well, I'm rising above it; that's what great men do. Rise above adversity. Besides, I'm too busy to obsess about the unfairness of life, because I'm working all the time.

I work at Amalgamated Waste Management from twelve-thirty to five p.m. on Saturdays and school holidays. 'Nuff said. It's not that bad. Mostly because I think I fried whatever sense receptors in my nasal cavity used to allow me to smell. I think I'll ask to stay on even after I've worked off my bill. An honest job is a great thing, I've discovered.

I work from five-thirty to nine-thirty p.m. on Saturdays and school holidays at the storage facility, cleaning out abandoned spaces, inventorying items for sale and dividing the rest into resale, recycle and refuse.

It's pretty good money. Nowadays I work hard and there's nothing, *ab-sew-loot-lee nuh-thing*, smart about what I do. But maybe eighth graders weren't meant to be world-class moguls.

I'm as confident as ever that success is still in my future. A guy like me can't help but excel in this life, even if I'm taking a break from the fast track right now.

I never did manage to ask Tina out on a date. I was at work the night of the dance. She still doesn't know I'm the best possible boyfriend material in the whole entire school.

I have new ideas for how to fix that. I just know that the very next time I come up with a plan to get her attention, it's going to work.

Gary Paulsen is the distinguished author of many critically acclaimed books for young people, including three Newbery Honor Books: *The Winter Room, Hatchet,* and *Dogsong.* He won the Margaret A. Edwards Award given by the ALA for his lifetime achievement in young adult literature. Among his Random House books are *Liar, Liar; Woods Runner; Lawn Boy; Lawn Boy Returns; Notes from the Dog; Mudshark; The Legend of Bass Reeves; The Amazing Life of Birds; The Time Hackers; Molly McGinty Has a Really Good Day; The Quilt* (a companion to *Alida's Song* and *The Cookcamp*); *How Angel Peterson Got His Name; Guts: The True Stories Behind* Hatchet *and the Brian Books; The Beet Fields; Soldier's Heart; Brian's Return, Brian's Winter,* and *Brian's Hunt* (companions to *Hatchet*); *Father Water, Mother Woods;* and five books about Francis Tucket's adventures in the Old West. Gary Paulsen has also published fiction and nonfiction for adults. His wife, Ruth Wright Paulsen, is an artist who has illustrated several of his books. He divides his time between his home in Alaska, his ranch in New Mexico, and his sailboat on the Pacific Ocean. You can visit him on the Web at GaryPaulsen.com.

Here's another terrific story about Kevin

LiAR, LiaR

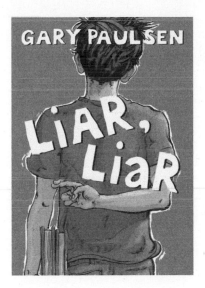

Available from Wendy Lamb Books
ISBN: 978-0-385-74001-2